THE HUNDRED AND ONE DALMATIANS

by
Dodie Smith

Adapted by Peter Bently
Illustrated by Steven Lenton

Abrams Books for Young Readers • New York

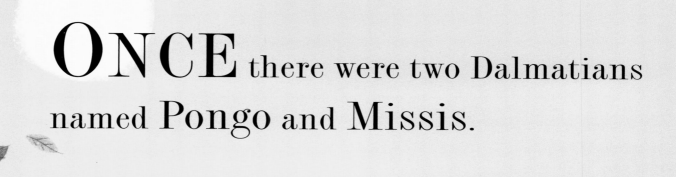

ONCE there were two Dalmatians named Pongo and Missis.

They lived with Mr. and Mrs. Dearly in a big house in London.

"Guess what, Pongo?" said Missis one day. "We are going to have **puppies!**"

But Missis didn't have just **one** puppy.

Or two.

Or three.

She had **fifteen!**

The biggest puppy was Patch. He looked after tiny Cadpig, the smallest puppy of all.

Lucky was the bravest.

And Roly-Poly made everyone laugh.

One afternoon, a woman came to the house.
Her name was **Cruella de Vil.**

"What delightful dogs!"
declared Cruella.
"I will buy **them all.**"

"We'll never
sell them," said
Mr. Dearly firmly.

"Pity," muttered Cruella as she left.
"They would make an enchanting fur coat."

Pongo **growled**.

"I don't like Cruella de Vil," he said.

"Nor do I," said Missis. "She's mean enough
to scare the spots off a pup!"

Not long afterward, Pongo
and Missis went out for a walk,
but when they returned . . .

. . . the puppies were gone!

"Perhaps they're
hiding," said Pongo.

But they were
nowhere in the house.

"My poor pups have been **stolen!**" wailed Missis.

Mr. and Mrs. Dearly called the police.

They put ads in the newspapers.

But it was no use. The puppies had vanished!

That evening, Pongo and Missis sat on
a nearby hill and barked.

"Help!" they cried.
"Fifteen Dalmatian
puppies stolen!"

Many dogs heard them.
But no one had
seen the puppies.

But then, from far away, they heard an old sheepdog.
"I have seen your puppies," he barked gruffly.
"They are at an old mansion in the countryside!"

"We must go there and rescue
them!" said Missis.

"You're right!" said Pongo. "We will leave tonight!"

When the Dearlys were asleep, Pongo and Missis
snuck out of the house.

They ran through the freezing streets and into the countryside.
On and on they went, through sleeping villages and frosty fields.

At last, they reached the mansion. The old sheepdog
greeted them warmly. His name was the Colonel.

"What a terrifying place!" said Missis.

"It belongs to a woman named Cruella de Vil," said the Colonel.

"I knew it!" said Pongo. "Cruella stole our puppies!"

The house was surrounded by a high wall.
How would the dogs get in?

The Colonel knew a way. He led Pongo
and Missis into an old tower.

When they reached the top,
Missis looked out and gasped.

She could see her puppies—
and dozens more!

"Cruella has been collecting
Dalmatian puppies," said the Colonel.
"She wants to make them all
into spotty fur coats."

"Then we must save them all!" said Missis.

Two men came out of the house.
"That's Saul and Jasper," said the Colonel.
"They are guarding the pups for Cruella.
But they spend most of their time
watching TV."

That evening, Pongo and Missis crept up to the house.
"There's Lucky!" cried Missis.

"Mom! Dad!" exclaimed Lucky.
"We knew you'd rescue us!

Come on, I'll take
you to the others.
If we're quiet, Saul and Jasper
won't notice a thing."

Suddenly, they heard a voice outside the door.

"Saul!
Jasper!
Where are you?"

Pongo and Missis froze. They had heard that voice before . . .

It was **Cruella de Vil!**

"The whole country is looking for those pups!" snarled Cruella. "I want you to make them into spotty fur coats tonight!" She slammed the door and went upstairs to bed.

"It'll take ages to round up all the pups!" grumbled Jasper. "Let's watch some more TV first."

"Now's our chance to escape," whispered Pongo. He and Missis led the puppies out through a kitchen window.

On the way out, they ate everything in sight. "Cruella won't have any breakfast!" laughed Pongo.

"Serves her right," said Missis.

Soon the Dalmatians climbed
out of the tower and escaped to the
other side of the wall.

"Cruella is sure to come after you," said the Colonel.
"You must leave now."

"It's a long way home," frowned Missis. "The puppies are too small to walk all that way. Especially Cadpig."

"Don't worry," smiled the old sheepdog. "Cadpig can ride in this wagon!"

"Good idea," said Pongo.

"Thanks for your help!" said Missis.

"My pleasure," said the Colonel. "Goodbye—and good luck!"

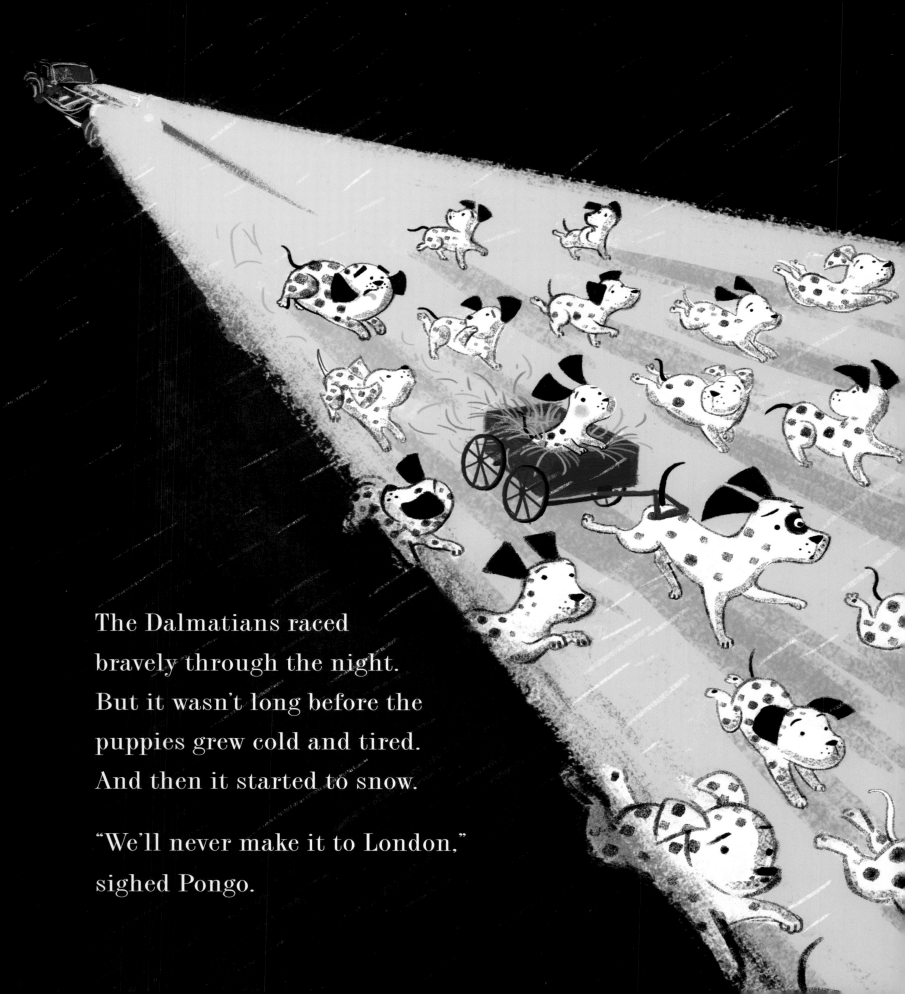

The Dalmatians raced
bravely through the night.
But it wasn't long before the
puppies grew cold and tired.
And then it started to snow.

"We'll never make it to London,"
sighed Pongo.

TOOT! TOOT!
"That's Cruella's car!" cried Missis.
"It's coming this way!"

Cruella was getting closer. But there was nowhere to hide.

Then Missis spotted a big van parked nearby. And sitting in the back of the van was a little terrier.

"Help!" barked Pongo.
"We're being chased!"

"You're the missing Dalmatians!" said the terrier. "Quick, jump in!"
The Dalmatians scrambled into the van just in time.

Cruella zoomed
right past them . . .

"Look!" cried Missis. "She's skidding!"

C R A S H

Cruella's car slid off the
road into a ditch.

"You're safe now!" cheered the terrier.

"My driver's heading to London. Need a ride?"

"Yes, please!" said Pongo and Missis.

It was snowing heavily outside when
Mr. and Mrs. Dearly heard barking.

They dashed to the door—
and in ran dozens of Dalmatians!

"It's Pongo and Missis and their puppies!" cried Mr. Dearly.

"And many more puppies, too!" said Mrs. Dearly.

They started to count them all.

As the Dearlys finished counting, the clock struck midnight.

"It's Christmas!" said Mrs. Dearly.

"Well done, Pongo and Missis!"

"We've got the best
Christmas present ever.

One
hundred
and one
Dalmatians!"

For Tara, who loves dogs
—P.B.

For the stupendous Steven Butler x
—S.L.

Cataloging-in-Publication Data has been applied for and may be obtained from the Library of Congress.

Library of Congress Control Number 2018966464
ISBN 978-1-4197-3632-2

Originally published by Egmont UK Ltd.
Original text copyright © Pongo and Missis Ltd 1956
Text adaptation copyright © Pongo and Missis Ltd 2017
Text adapted by Peter Bently from the original title *The Hundred and One Dalmatians* written by Dodie Smith
Illustrations copyright © Steven Lenton 2017
Steven Lenton has asserted his moral rights. All rights reserved.

Book design by Max Temescu

Printed and bound in Malaysia
10 9 8 7 6 5 4 3 2 1

Abrams Books for Young Readers are available at special discounts when purchased in quantity for premiums and promotions as well as fundraising or educational use. Special editions can also be created to specification. For details, contact specialsales@abramsbooks.com or the address below.

Abrams® is a registered trademark of Harry N. Abrams, Inc.

ABRAMS The Art of Books
195 Broadway, New York, NY 10007
abramsbooks.com

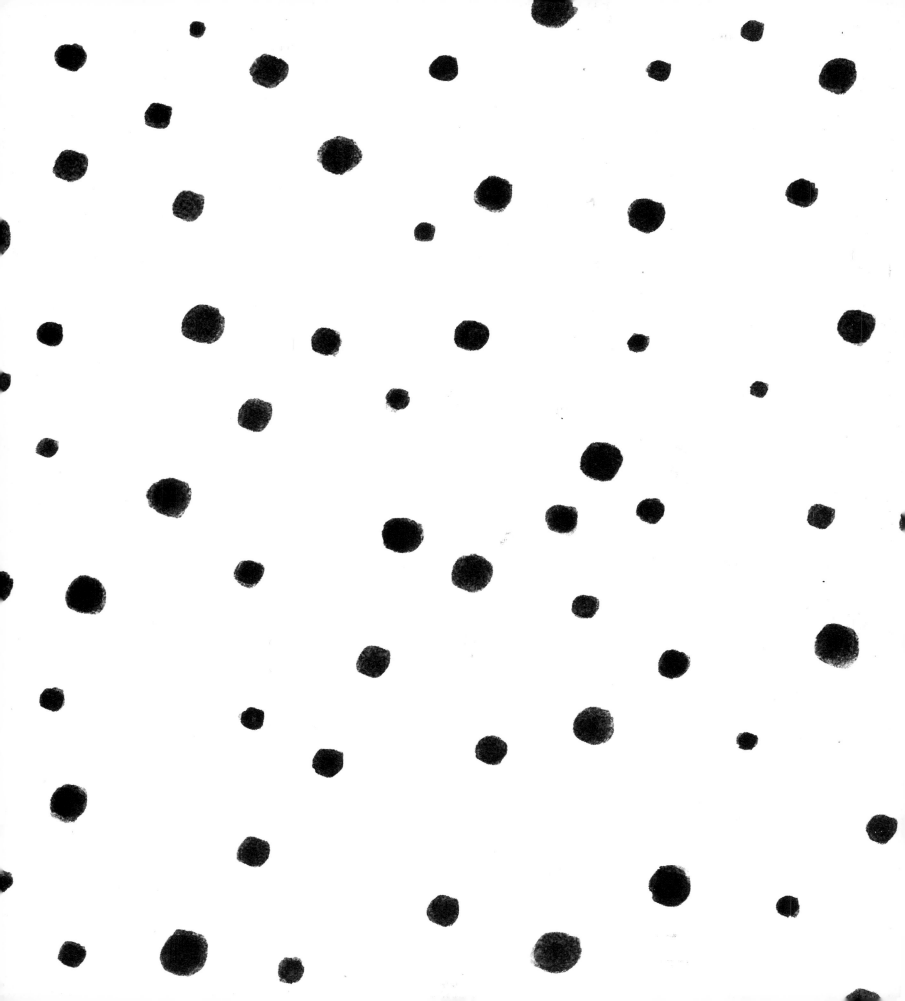